D0345252

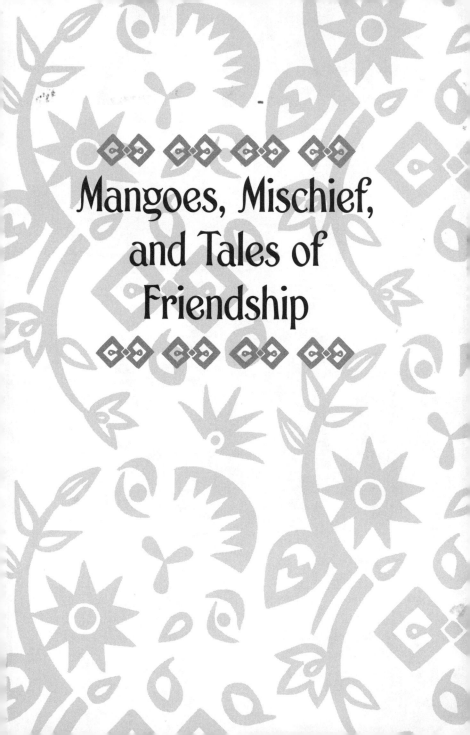

Mangoes, Mischief, and Tales of Friendship

Chitra Soundar, author.
Mangoes, mischief, and tales of
friendship
2019

cu   04/03/19

Mangoes, Mischief, and Tales of Friendship

❖❖ ❖❖ ❖❖ ❖❖

CHITRA SOUNDAR

illustrated by UMA KRISHNASWAMY

CANDLEWICK PRESS

This is a work of fiction. Names, characters, places,
and incidents are either products of the author's imagination
or, if real, are used fictitiously.

A Dollop of Ghee and a Pot of Wisdom
Text copyright © 2010 by Chitra Soundar
Illustrations copyright © 2010 by Uma Krishnaswamy

A Jar of Pickles and a Pinch of Justice
Text copyright © 2016 by Chitra Soundar
Illustrations copyright © 2016 by Uma Krishnaswamy

All rights reserved. No part of this book may be reproduced,
transmitted, or stored in an information retrieval system in any
form or by any means, graphic, electronic, or mechanical,
including photocopying, taping, and recording, without
prior written permission from the publisher.

First U.S. edition 2019

Library of Congress Catalog Card Number pending
ISBN 978-1-5362-0067-6

18 19 20 21 22 23 LSC 10 9 8 7 6 5 4 3 2 1

Printed in Crawfordsville, IN, U.S.A.

This book was typeset in Stempel Schneidler.
The illustrations were done in acrylic, poster color,
and watercolor.

Candlewick Press
99 Dover Street
Somerville, Massachusetts 02144

visit us at www.candlewick.com

Contents

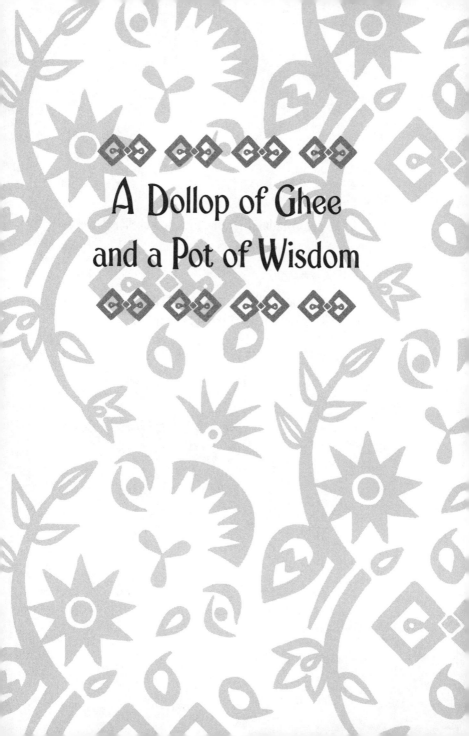

A Dollop of Ghee and a Pot of Wisdom

To my grandmother, my first storyteller
C. S.

To Jacky Paynter, the designer,
for quiet support, thoughtful insights
U. K.

Contents

Prince Veera's First Case

Long ago in a faraway land, King Bheema ruled a small kingdom surrounded by the magnificent hills of Himtuk. King Bheema was a kind and just ruler. Every day he held court at the palace. Rich or poor, tall or short, man or woman—anyone could walk in with a problem. The king would always find a way to solve it.

The king lived with his wife and son in a red stone palace. Prince Veera was ten years old. But he didn't go to school—the school came to him. His teachers lived in the palace and taught him mathematics, science, economics, and many languages, including Persian, Mandarin, and Latin.

The prince had to master archery, horseback riding, and swimming. Sons of ministers and students with special scholarships came to the palace to study with him.

If anyone could compete with Prince Veera, it was Suku, the farmer's son. Suku had won a scholarship to study with the prince. He was a good match for Veera and could best him in wrestling and fencing. He rode horses as well as Veera, too.

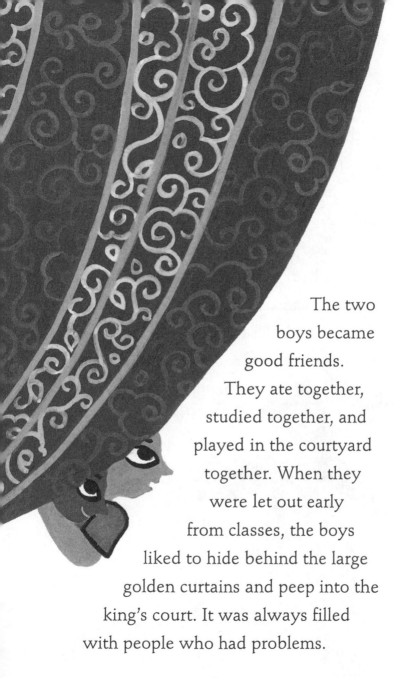

The two
boys became
good friends.
They ate together,
studied together, and
played in the courtyard
together. When they
were let out early
from classes, the boys
liked to hide behind the large
golden curtains and peep into the
king's court. It was always filled
with people who had problems.

Three days after
harvest, Suku came
to the palace to
see Prince Veera. He
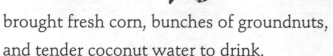
brought fresh corn, bunches of groundnuts,
and tender coconut water to drink.

"Do you want to go to the woods?" Prince
Veera asked. "We can check mongoose holes
for snakes and chase deer and bison."

"After a week of harvest, I don't want to
be anywhere near plants and trees," said
Suku. "Can we sneak
into the court and see
what's going on?"

"Let's go to the queen's chambers," said Veera. "We can watch the court through the small windows."

The boys scampered through the rooms, jumping onto ornate chests. The thick carpets hid the sound of their hurrying feet. Whenever a guard appeared, they hid behind the large carved doors. As soon as they reached the queen's chambers, Veera peeked in to see if any of his mother's maids were there with the flowers and perfume the queen needed for her bath.

Seeing no one, the boys went through the recreation room and into the viewing gallery. The long, thin corridor overlooked the court. Alongside the windows, a bench was set up for the queen to sit on and listen. The round windows were decorated with carvings of peacocks and elephants. They glistened, reflecting the sparkle of the gemstones.

"This is a great place to spy," said Prince Veera. "You can see and hear everything that happens."

"Shh!" Suku whispered. "Spies don't chatter."

Before Veera could reply, a horn blared. He and Suku kneeled on the cushioned benches and peeped through the windows. To the beat of drums, King Bheema entered through the large doors. Two soldiers walked in front of him. A long train of maroon silk stretched from the king's tunic.

"What if the sentry steps on it?" Prince Veera asked.

"I'll die laughing," said Suku.

"I'm sure you *will* die if you laugh," said Prince Veera. "Want to try?"

"Shh! Stop talking," said Suku.

From below they heard the king say, "Let the proceedings begin."

Then King Bheema sat down on his throne.

A man stepped to the center of the court and gave his name. He asked the king to do something about the crows that dirtied his newly built terrace.

As people presented their problems, the king sometimes asked them to come back later with more details or to bring a witness. Sometimes he gave them work, sometimes he gave them money. One or two even got punished for wasting his time.

Some of the problems were serious. One man was there about his sick parents. A woman came to complain about her greedy landlord.

Some people had silly problems—like the man who had lost his shadow. Another wanted to charge rent to the birds that sat on his roof. A woman came to complain that the roadside tree gave more shade to her neighbor's house than her own.

"That's ridiculous," said Suku when a man asked if he could live inside his neighbor's chimney.

"I'm sure *we* could solve these problems," said Veera.

"And who's going to let us?" Suku said.

That evening the boys didn't play in the woods or swim in the river. They played court instead. Prince Veera met imaginary people and heard their cases. Suku was his counsel.

A week had
gone by. There were no classes
on New Moon day. With nothing to do, the
boys crept into the palace to watch King
Bheema hold court.

But this time, the court was empty, and
outside there was a long line of people
waiting to see the king.

"Where is your father?" Suku asked.

Veera and Suku raced to the king's
chambers.

"The king is unwell," said the royal
physician. "Don't bother him."

Veera looked at his father's pale face.
His mother, the queen, sat close by,
tending to him.

"But people are waiting," Veera whispered to Suku.

"Maybe we should open our own court," Suku whispered back.

Veera's eyes twinkled. "This is the perfect opportunity."

He leaned toward his father's bed. "Father, I can hold court today on your behalf," he said.

"What?" the king sputtered, trying to sit up.

"We have been listening to your court for many days," admitted Veera. "We're sure we can handle it."

"Are you trying to become king?" asked the king, smiling.

"No, Father, but I will learn to govern," said Veera, "and you can get some rest."

11

"Well, that sounds very tempting," the king said. "But you can't do this on your own."

"Here I present to you my wise counsel, Suku," said Veera.

The king smiled at both of them. "You've been planning this for a long time then," he said. "Very well. I'll give you a chance. But you can hear only simple cases and only in the courtyard. Not in my court."

"Anything you say, Father," Veera said, unable to hide his smile.

A court was
set up quickly in the courtyard. Prince
Veera's chair was placed in the middle.
A chair for Suku was placed to its right.
Four sentries stood nearby, guarding the
courtyard as people formed a line. Some
people were alone, some had brought their
friends. Some were empty-handed. Some
held chickens or eggs, and one even held a
bucket of *biriyani.*

A sentry announced the arrival of the
prince. A loud gasp rose from the people.
"Where is the king?" many of them cried.

13

"Let's hear the first case," said the prince, sitting down.

A man who smelled of hay stepped forward and bowed to the prince. "Your Highness," he began, "my neighbor follows my cow all around town and picks up the cow dung. I want you to forbid him to do that. Anything that the cow drops belongs to me."

Veera thought about it for a moment and said, "From today, why don't you tie a dung bag behind the cow? Then you can collect all the droppings yourself."

"Next case!" said Suku.

"Dear Prince," said the next man who stepped forward. "It's my neighbor. I want her to stop singing."

"Is she awful?" asked Veera.

"She is the best singer in this city, Your Highness," he explained. "I just sit next to the window all day and listen. I miss work on most days."

Veera and Suku huddled and discussed the case.

"From today onward, you have to keep your windows shut until you come back from work," Veera ordered.

"Who is next?" asked Suku.

Two men stepped forward. One was dressed in cotton and the other in silk. The first man stood with his arms folded. The second man leaned on his wooden cane and stroked his mustache.

"State your case," said Prince Veera.

"With due respect, dear Prince, I think this problem is too tricky for you," said the second man.

"If I decide the problem is too big for me, the king will surely talk to you tomorrow," said the prince. "Today you must place your trust in me."

"My name is Meetaram," said the second man. "I have a small sweetshop in the market. I make all the sweets myself and I use only pure butter and sugar."

"This is the prince's court. Don't waste our time talking about your sweetshop," said Suku.

"I really like sweets," said the prince. "I want to hear more."

"Your Majesty, we make *laddus, jalebis,* and *kheer* and *soan papdi.* We make all sorts of sweets. We are famous all over the kingdom."

"Have you brought any sweets with you?" asked the prince.

Meetaram turned and gestured to someone. Another man entered and handed

Meetaram a large plate covered by a
checked cloth. The smell of sugar and butter
wafted over the courtyard. The people
closed their eyes and enjoyed the smell.

"Very nice!" said the
prince. "It smells
very nice." He
leaned forward
to take a sweet.

Suku shook
his head ever
so slightly.
Veera sat back in his chair,
frowning at Suku.

"Don't smell it, Your Majesty,"
said the other man. "That's
exactly the problem."

"Take the sweets to my
room," Veera said.

A sentry took the plate from Meetaram.

"Your Majesty," said Meetaram, "this

man, Kapi, stood several minutes outside my shop smelling my sweets. But he left without buying or paying."

"If he didn't buy, why must he pay?" asked Veera.

"Because he enjoyed the smell so much. It takes a lot of butter and sugar to get that smell, Your Majesty. That smell attracts many customers into the shop. If they all came just to smell my sweets and never buy any, I wouldn't make any money."

"Hmmm, interesting," said the prince.

"This man Kapi should pay five silver coins for enjoying the sweet smells in my shop. You have to be fair, Prince Veera, just like your father."

Prince Veera closed his eyes. He could almost touch the wafting fragrance of the sweets. It made him slightly hungry.

"Kapi, what do you say for yourself?"

Kapi was not as richly dressed as Meetaram. He was thin and didn't wear any jewelry. His white shirt was almost brown and his dhoti was patched in many places.

"My dear prince, I'm a poor man," Kapi began. "I work very hard in the fields. Once a month, I come to town to buy groceries. I have only five silver coins. Walking through the market, I smelled the sweets. I stopped for a few minutes, taking in the wonderful smells. But the sweets were too expensive. I couldn't afford to buy rice, vegetables, *and* sweets with the money I had."

"What did you do then?" asked the prince. He didn't realize that people had to choose between vegetables and sweets. He was surprised that Kapi decided to buy vegetables instead of sweets. *I'd definitely choose the sweets,* he thought.

"My children need food, Your Majesty. They go to school and they need to eat well. The sweets would last for just a day. But the rice and vegetables will last all month. So I decided not to buy the sweets."

"But you enjoyed the smell?" the prince asked.

"Yes, I did. Somehow the smell itself was enough. It felt like eating the sweets."

"That's exactly my case, Your Majesty," piped in Meetaram.

"Shh!" Suku hushed the man.

The prince closed his eyes. He tried not to think about the sweets, just the problem in front of him. What would his father do?

"OK, I've decided," said Prince Veera. "Kapi, give your five silver coins to Meetaram."

Kapi's face fell. With tears in his eyes, he handed over the money.

Meetaram's face lit up with joy. He counted the five silver coins at least five times.

The prince watched this in silence.

"Thank you, dear Prince. You are very fair and just," said Meetaram. "I'll take my leave now."

"Not so fast, my man. Now please return the five silvers to Kapi."

"But—"

"Well, he smelled your sweets, but he didn't eat them."

"Yes, but—"

"And you held the money in your hands, didn't you?"

"Yes, but—"

"You counted it; you imagined adding it to your money box. You enjoyed that, didn't you?"

"Yes, but—"

"He enjoyed the smell of sweets, and you enjoyed the feel of money. A fair exchange, don't you think?"

Meetaram hung his head in shame.

"From now on, treat your customers fairly," Prince Veera cautioned. "Always make some sweets for people who cannot afford to buy expensive ones."

Meetaram returned the money and left the court.

"Bring the plate of sweets from my room," said the prince. "Take these to your children, Kapi. Let them eat rice, vegetables, *and* sweets today."

Kapi left the court smiling and carrying a large basket filled with sweets.

That night during dinner, Prince Veera ate all his vegetables, even his peas.

Who Stole the *Laddus?*

Ever since Meetaram brought the sweets into the court, not a meal was eaten without discussing them. The cooks, sentries, maids — everyone talked about the sweets and the fragrance that lingered in the hallways.

"Maybe the prince should have given the sweets to everyone," said a sentry.

"Maybe the prince should have fined Meetaram and made him bring more sweets," said another.

Prince Veera, too, found it difficult to forget the aroma of the sweets. He ordered that the palace be sprayed with camphor fumes to wipe out the wafting smell. But it didn't help. The smell was lodged in everyone's minds. Wiping it out of the courtyard, thrones, curtains, and carpets didn't make it go away.

The news reached the ministers, then the queen and king.

"What is this gossip about sweets?" King Bheema asked.

"It's nothing, Father. Just a case," said Prince Veera.

"Was the smell really divine?" asked the queen.

"Yes, it was. Not even the royal cook has made sweets that smelled like that."

"Your father loves sweets," said the queen. "Especially those made of butter! The *laddus,* that's his favorite."

"Maybe we should order some sweets," said the king. "If only I'd handled this case before I let you have your own court!"

"Let me check that Meetaram is not cheating anyone now. If he has reformed his ways, then you can buy sweets from his shop," Prince Veera said. He didn't want Meetaram to use his court to sell more sweets.

So the next day, the prince set off to the market dressed like an urchin.

"Can you find the shop on your own?" asked the queen.

"I'll ask around," said Prince Veera. But he didn't have to. The buttery, sugary smell wafted through the market, telling him where to go.

Veera sat outside the sweetshop for hours, smelling the cinnamon, cardamom, and cashews. He watched the customers come in and saw that Meetaram was fair to them. He looked at the plates on the shelves, loaded with sweets. He licked his lips but he bought nothing.

After sunset Meetaram closed his shop
and Prince Veera returned to the palace,
hungry, tired, and hot. It is hard business,
this justice, he thought. But it was good to
know that Meetaram had indeed mended
his ways.

The next day, the prince sent a sentry
with a large cart down to the market. The
king had written down his order for the
sweets and so had the queen. Prince Veera
and Suku wanted some, too. Every member
of the royal household wanted the sweets.

Meetaram was delighted. He checked the
list many times. He loaded the cart with
sweets. "These are for the king, the queen,
and the prince," he said. "I will personally
deliver the rest by tomorrow. First we have
to make a new batch."

"That means the rest of us will have to
wait another day," said the sentry, and he
drove the cart back toward the palace.

Back at the palace, the royal family was
waiting. As soon as the cart arrived, the
sweets were unloaded and brought to the
kitchen.

The king stepped forward and opened a
large box of *laddus*. The yellow balls of lentils

fried in sugar syrup glistened
in the light.

"*Svadishta!*
Delicious!" he
cried, after biting
into a big *laddu*.

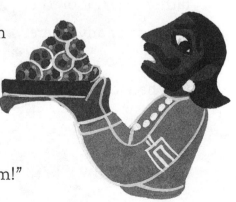

Just as he finished the first and reached
for a second, the minister arrived. "A
messenger from the kingdom of Chalu is
here to see you, Your Majesty," he said.

"Not now!" the king moaned.

"Sorry, Your Majesty. This is of utmost
importance."

The king put the box down
on the table. There
were exactly eleven
laddus left. "Don't
smell them and
don't touch
them," he warned.
"And don't eat them!"

* * *

Early the next morning, Prince Veera was
awakened by a loud noise. He stumbled
out of bed and went to the door. What
was it? It was not thunder, but more like
a roar. He opened the door and listened
intently. It sounded like his father. But King
Bheema never shouted—at least, not that
early in the morning! The sun had not even
risen high enough to warm the pond in the
garden.

Prince Veera slipped out of his room and
followed the sound. His father was not in
his room. He was not in the courtyard. His
father was not on the
grounds or anywhere
near the pond.

Where could
he be?

Prince Veera
listened hard.

The sound came from the far east wing of the palace, by the royal kitchen. What was his father doing in the kitchen? He hardly ever went there, unless he didn't want anyone to know he was eating.

Then Veera remembered the sweets, the sweets that his father had to abandon until his official duties were over! Veera walked swiftly to the kitchen.

A crowd of servants stood outside, their ears to the door. Inside, the king ranted and raved. When Prince Veera walked closer, the servants moved away.

"What's going on?" Veera asked.

"It's about the *laddu*," said one of the maids.

"The *laddu*? Is that the reason for his anger?"

I handled the case and I brought the fragrance into the palace, Veera thought. *Oh, my sweet butters, what's going to happen to me?*

"One *laddu* is missing," said the maid. "The king left exactly eleven of them in the box last night. This morning, when he came by, only ten remained."

"Do you know who took the missing *laddu*?"

"No one knows. Nobody will own up."

Prince Veera smiled. This was something he could handle. Well, the *laddu* had gone missing. It would never come back,

but the memory of its fragrance and its taste would never leave the mind of the person who had eaten it. "Time for me to sort this out," he said as he pushed the door open and went into the kitchen.

Inside he saw that the king was still in his pajamas, standing on top of a huge cauldron. His face was red. The kitchen staff stood in front of him, shaking like flags on a windy day.

"Father, what is the problem?" Veera asked.

The king stopped his tirade and looked at his son. "I want to know who is lying. I can forgive stealing, but not lying."

"Why not leave this to me?" said the prince. "I'll find out."

"This is all because of your case," said the king. "We were happy before we knew about Meetaram's sweets."

Prince Veera hung his head. The sooner he found the culprit,

the better it
would be for
everyone.

He braced
himself and
looked up.
"Father, you
have many

appointments today. Why don't you get ready while I solve this problem? I'll bring the culprit to your court."

King Bheema handed the box of *laddus* to his guard and said, "Keep this under lock and key."

Prince Veera smiled. "Remember," he said to everyone. "You are in this kitchen to cook food, not steal it. The sooner we get to the bottom of this, the sooner we can all get back to cooking breakfast and lunch."

No one stirred. The thief was lying low.

"I know the sweets are very tempting and the smell makes you hungry, but it is not good to lie to the king," said Prince Veera. "Now, who took the *laddu*?"

No one would own up. Not a single word was spoken. Prince Veera didn't know who the thief could be.

"I'll tell the king to forgive you," said the prince, "but you must confess now."

Again no one stepped forward.

"Then it is time to invoke the God of Honesty," the prince said, signaling to the sentry. "Please fetch me twenty pieces of firewood of the same length."

In a few minutes, the sentry returned with an armload of firewood.

"Each of you gets one piece of wood," said the prince. "You will step through the pantry invoking the God of Honesty and pray for mercy. Then you will come out the other side."

Everyone nodded.

"If you are speaking the truth, your firewood will shrink by an inch by the time you step out on the other side. If you are

lying, the God of Honesty will not grace
you with his presence and your stick will
remain the same length."

The sentry handed out the sticks as each
person walked through the pantry. The
prince stood waiting on the other side.

As they walked in, each of them
chanted the familiar slogan—"*Satyameva
Jayete!*"—invoking the God of Honesty.
Then they stepped out of the pantry and
stood in front of the prince with their piece
of wood.

"Measure each of these," Veera ordered.

The sentry measured each piece of firewood and noted the measurements on a scroll.

Prince Veera then read through the scroll and smiled. "I know who did it. Tell the king we will be in his court shortly."

But the king didn't wait for Veera. He wanted to know who had lied to him. He came to the kitchen right away.

"Do you know who did it?" asked the king.

"Yes, Father. I know who stole the *laddu* and who lied to us," said the prince.

"I'll forgive the stealing. The *laddu* is not important. We're getting another cartload today. But who lied to me?"

"The fourth man from the right," said Prince Veera.

Before the king could say anything, the liar fell at the king's feet. "I am sorry, Your Majesty. I won't lie to you ever again."

"Take him away, we'll deal with him

later," said the king. "How did you find this out, Veera?"

"I merely invoked the conscience of the guilty man," Prince Veera said.

"Did you threaten him?" asked the king.

"Father, I did no such thing," said Veera, and he explained what he had made the servants do.

"How did that help? Did the guilty man confess?"

"No, Father. The servants believed that the God of Honesty would shrink their firewood if they were innocent. Because the God of Honesty would not help him, the guilty man was afraid that his firewood would be longer than the others."

The king nodded with his eyes closed. He understood the minds of wrongdoers. They always lived in fear of being found out.

"The culprit took a knife and chopped a small bit of the firewood. So when we measured all of the pieces at the end, the one with the shortest firewood was the liar." Prince Veera held up the scroll.

"Well done, my son. The *laddu* thief was caught by his own guilty conscience."

"So can I share a *laddu* with you, Father?" Veera asked.

"Of course you can, my son," the king said. "Can I share one of your *jalebis*?"

The Case of the Greedy Moneylender

Prince Veera had a busy schedule during the day. He had to get up very early to go swimming. After breakfast he studied mathematics, science, and economics. After lunch he practiced archery, horseback riding, and wrestling.

One Wednesday, Suku was expected to join Veera for his morning swim. Veera waited at the riverbank, but there was no sign of his friend. Veera swam alone.

He expected Suku to join him for breakfast, but again he was disappointed.

"Where is Suku?" Veera asked his mother.

"Maybe he is needed at the farm today, son," said the queen.

The whole day passed and there was no sign of Suku. Veera couldn't wait any longer. He decided to go find him.

Veera rode his white horse through the wide streets of Himpur. His personal guards  rode behind him. The streets were lined with neem and banyan trees. Veera went past the village temple and the

lotus lake, and
then he crossed
the bridge
over the lake.
The streets were
narrower now and
the houses smaller.
Large corn and paddy
fields were dotted with farmhouses.

"Look, the prince is here
to see Suku," said a man
looking up from his work.

The people who lived
in Suku's neighborhood were
not surprised. Veera came often to visit
Suku and spent a lot of time playing in the
streets. If he was not wearing expensive
clothes or jewelry, or if there were no
guards around the area, they would not
realize it was Prince Veera playing hide-and-
seek on the streets with the other boys.

Veera dismounted from his horse outside
Suku's parents' house. He knocked on the
door and Suku's father opened it.

"Welcome, my dear prince," said
Suku's father.

"Good evening, sir. Where is
my friend Suku?" asked the
prince.

"He has gone away on a
short trip," said Suku's father.

"What sort of trip?"
asked the prince. "He never
mentioned anything."

"It was quite sudden, Your
Majesty. He had to leave this
morning."

50

Prince Veera looked around. Suku's clothes were still there. His bag and shoes were there, too. "All his things are here," he said. "Please tell me what is going on."

Suku's father couldn't hold back his tears any longer. "The greedy moneylender has taken my boy away, Your Majesty. I didn't want to burden you with my problems. Neither did Suku."

"How much do you owe the moneylender?" asked Prince Veera.

"Twenty-five silvers. Just twenty-five silvers. But I don't have that money. And I won't until I complete my harvest and sell my crops in the market."

"Who is this moneylender?" asked the prince. "He is very heartless."

"Angar is his name," said Suku's father, and he explained.

"Angar comes from a family of moneylenders. He charges heavy interest on the money he lends. He even leases utensils and jewelry for weddings. And he takes away people's belongings when they

are unable to pay the interest. He is very greedy, Your Majesty."

"I'm going to do something about this," said the prince.

"But Suku is still with him," said Suku's father. "I don't want to cause any trouble. I don't want anything to happen to my son, Your Majesty."

"Get me a bag of twenty-five silvers," Veera said to his guard, "and get my friend back." Then, to Suku's parents he said, "I'll teach the moneylender a lesson he will never forget."

Suku's parents refused the money at first, but Prince Veera urged them to take it. After a lot of discussion, they finally agreed to accept the prince's help in bringing their son back.

The next day Suku returned home from the moneylender's, then headed straight to the palace with a bag of sweet potatoes and guavas.

"Thank you," he said. "You have been very kind to us. My father will repay the money after the harvest."

"Never mind, Suku," said Prince Veera. "I couldn't wait until the harvest to beat you at horseback riding or archery, could I?"

"Ha! To be beaten, you mean!" said Suku. "You can't wait to lose."

"We'll see about that. What happened at the moneylender's house?" asked the prince. "Did he hurt you at all?"

"No, he just made me do all his chores," said Suku. "He made me count the money, make tea for him, and even wash his clothes. But that was easy. He had only two shirts and two dhotis."

"Didn't you say he was rich?"

"Yes, he is. But he doesn't spend money. He eats only one meal a day, to save his silvers."

"That is pure greed," said Prince Veera. "Maybe he is saving the money for a reason."

"I don't think any reason is good enough to swindle people out of their possessions," said Suku. "He makes people give up their hard-earned things and money just to fill his coffers."

"Does he have any children?"

"No children, no family," said Suku. "Not even a pet. He lives alone, counts his money, eats, sleeps, and snores. He doesn't even have anyone to collect his dues. If people return the money late, he charges more interest."

"We have to teach him a lesson, my friend," said Prince Veera. "We can't let him continue to cheat anymore."

"You mean, report him to your father's court?" asked Suku. "I don't think we can do that. People who borrow from him sign a paper that says they agree to his terms. Your father will throw the case out when he sees the papers."

"But that's not fair," said the prince. "We have to teach him a lesson. How about a bit of Veera treatment? Are you ready for some fun?"

Then Veera whispered a plan to his friend.

The next day, dressed as an ordinary farmer's boy, Veera set off to see the moneylender. No one noticed him as he walked down the street

56

and turned right
at the village square,
onto a road lined with
beautiful magnolia trees.

The fragrance was wonderful.

Angar the moneylender lived at number seventy-seven. A large statue of a white

elephant stood
outside the
door. *No one
could miss that,*
thought Veera
as he knocked.

A thin, scrawny
man opened the door.

"I'm here to see Angar, the moneylender," said Veera.

"What for?" barked the man.

"To borrow some cookware for my sister's wedding."

"Come in," said the man.

Veera stepped inside. The house was
large and spacious, but he noticed that there
wasn't any furniture, except for a desk set
up on a dais. The seating area was covered
in silk. There wasn't a single chair to sit on.

The man climbed onto the dais and sat
down on the silk-covered floor.

"I am Angar," he said. "What kind of
pots and pans do you need?"

"Can I look at them and decide?"
asked Veera.

The moneylender pointed to a green door. Veera pushed it open and stepped inside a room filled with pots, pans, ladles, and cups. They were made of copper, bronze, and steel, and some were made of earthenware.

Veera took a selection of bronze vessels and stepped out again. He put them on the floor and said, "These are the ones I need."

"Very well then. You are taking ten pots. You must return them in the same condition in a week's time. You owe me three silvers now and two silvers when you return them." The moneylender wrote down the details in his notebook.

Veera signed the agreement and handed three silvers to the moneylender, then took his pots and left.

One week went by and then two. A whole month had passed and still Veera hadn't bothered to return the pots.

"I think we have waited long enough," said Suku. "We should return the pots to the moneylender."

"Angar must have forgotten about them by now," said Veera. "He hasn't sent anyone to get them."

"He doesn't do that," explained Suku. "He simply charges more. Make sure you bring some extra silvers with you."

"Don't worry, my friend," said Veera. "I have enough to keep Angar happy."

He carefully lifted twenty pots and placed them in a cart.

Suku drove the cart while Veera sat inside, holding the pots. The boys arrived at the moneylender's house and unloaded the cart.

On hearing them, Angar appeared from inside.

"Where were you all this time?" he yelled. "You should have returned these pots weeks ago. I will have to charge you more now."

Veera smiled. "Well, kind sir, there is a small problem. You asked me to return the pots in the same condition. But I'm afraid that is not possible."

"Why not? Did you break them? How did you break bronze pots?"

"I didn't break them," said Veera. "But, you see, these pots gave birth to little ones. They were in a delicate state. I couldn't bring them until the little pots were strong enough to travel."

"Strong enough?" asked the moneylender. "What are you talking about?"

"See, dear sir, you didn't realize that the pots you lent me were with children," explained Veera. "After the wedding was over, I left them in the pantry for just a few hours. Then I heard sounds. Sounds of the pots rattling and clanging. When I rushed in to check, there were little pots in them."

"I don't believe this," said Angar.

"I knew you'd say that," said the prince. "Here, I brought your pots with their little ones. They all belong to you rightfully."

Angar counted the big pots. There were ten. He counted the small pots. There were ten. Well, what a neat profit!

"Thank you, young man," he said. "You're very honest. Others would have hidden the little pots and never returned them."

Even though Angar was happy with the little pots, he still charged Veera for the delay in returning the large ones. Veera forked over five silvers and returned home with Suku.

"I couldn't believe it when he actually stroked the little pots with love," said Suku. "That man is so greedy."

"Let him enjoy his pots while he can," said Veera. His eyes glinted at the prospect of teaching Angar a lesson. No one mistreated his friend and got away with it!

A week later, again
dressed in ordinary clothes,
Veera set off to see the moneylender.
This time he needed no introduction. When
he asked for twenty pots, the moneylender
was more than happy to lend them.

"Please take as many as you like.
Remember to bring back any little ones," he
said, giving him a receipt for six silvers.

Veera returned home and sent the pots to
the royal kitchen. They weren't
going anywhere again. Suku and
Veera continued with their
lessons for a month before
they remembered Angar
and his pots.

"Now that we are done with our lessons, do you think Angar is ready for his?" Suku asked.

"That sounds like fun," said Veera, and they discussed what they would tell Angar.

Veera and Suku set off on their horses, but they dismounted before they reached Angar's house. They walked up to the door and knocked.

When the door opened, Veera and
Suku burst out crying. They sat on the
doorstep and cried loudly. They wailed and
screamed. The whole street came to watch.

"What's wrong with you?" asked Angar.
"Why are you crying?"

"It's about the pots. I can't bear to tell
you," said the prince.

"What about the pots?"

"You see, they are bronze pots. They
were very old."

"I know! They are my family heirlooms.
Irreplaceable. If I had to buy them now, it

would cost me at least five hundred silvers."

On hearing this, Veera and Suku sobbed more.

"Tell me what's wrong," Angar said.

"Do you remember these pots gave birth to the little ones last month?" asked Veera.

"I remember. What happened now?"

"Well, the pots must have been very ill. Didn't you take care of them properly? After we put them in the pantry, there was no noise. I went to check on them. But unfortunately they were all dead."

"Dead?"

"Yes, the pots died yesterday at dawn!" cried Veera. "I'm so sorry."

"How can the pots die? They are made of bronze." Angar threw up his hands in despair.

"Well, if they can give birth to little bronze pots, can't they die, too?" asked Suku.

Angar had no answer to this. He hung his head in shame. The whole street laughed at his misery.

From that day onward, Angar stopped being greedy. He charged fair interest and he never unjustly took away things—or children—from anyone again.

The Unfortunate Case

It was a hot summer. No one in the kingdom studied during the hottest months. The sun scorched the earth. Lakes and streams dried up. The children were allowed to play outdoors only until noon and then again at dusk. They had to remain indoors during the afternoon.

Prince Veera and Suku spent their time in the mangroves near the palace. The grove was shady and cool. The boys climbed trees, chased dragonflies, and

feasted on juicy mangoes.
A river ran right through
the grove that was fed
from the beautiful hills
of Himtuk and it
never dried up.
After a long
day of playing,
the boys were
tired. The sun
was setting
and it was the
right time to get
something to eat.
"Let's go to the palace
and raid the kitchen,"
said Veera.

"That's what we always
do," said Suku. "Why don't
we go to the marketplace
today?"

72

Prince Veera never turned down an opportunity to mingle with his people. He preferred to roam the streets rather than travel in style in a carriage.

"Let's do that," he said.

So the boys set off to the market with a silver coin each. A guard dressed in plain clothes followed them at a discreet distance.

The market was bustling with people. The stalls were filled with fruits, vegetables, sweets, and cold drinks.

One man sold tender coconut water and
another sold palm fruits. A woman sold
buttermilk from a huge mud pot.

People came to the market on horses
and donkeys and
in carts.

The sound of animals mingled with the noise of the vendors and the bells from the temple nearby.

Prince Veera enjoyed his visits to the market. It was much more exciting than the palace.

Suku and Veera wandered around, trying on hats, eating mangoes, and drinking coconut milk.

As they approached the village square, people were whispering.

Suku spotted a
man under a banyan
tree. The man was
dressed in rags and
he carried a
dirty cotton
bag.

"What
is it?" the
prince asked.
"Why are people whispering?"

"Nothing, my friend. Let's go to the other
street," Suku said, steering Veera away.
Then, *"Pschckkk!"*

Prince Veera turned and saw the look
of dismay on his friend's face. Veera burst
out laughing. Suku had stepped in horse
manure. He held up his leg and hopped
around. "You never watch where you
walk," Veera said.

"It's not my fault!" cried Suku. "It is all

because of the bad luck that man spreads."

"Why are you blaming a stranger, Suku?" asked Veera.

Suku didn't reply. He approached a nearby shop and asked the shopkeeper for a pot of water to clean his shoes. "Let's go," he said.

Even after they returned to the palace, Prince Veera couldn't help thinking about the incident at the market. "Are you going to tell me or not?" he asked. "Why did you blame the man from the market?"

"I don't want to share bad luck, Veera," said Suku. "Why don't you just let it go?"

"I thought you knew me better," said Veera.

"I will tell you then," said Suku. "The man's name is Dhuri. He spreads bad luck throughout the kingdom."

"How could someone spread bad luck?" asked Veera. "What does he do?"

"He does nothing. Just by seeing or talking to him, something bad will happen to you," Suku explained, still examining his shoes for specks of horse manure.

"I'm sure that is just superstition," said Veera.

"Not at all. I stepped in horse manure as soon as I saw him."

"That was because you never watch where you walk," said Veera. "You were slurping on the juicy mangoes."

"I don't agree," said Suku. "It's all bad luck. And that man is spreading it."

Prince Veera argued hard and long with Suku, but they got nowhere. "Let's ask my father," he suggested.

"Don't do that, Veera. The king will want to meet this man. What if something bad happens to the king?"

"A king should meet all his subjects," said the prince. "He cannot discriminate."

So they took their problem to the king.
King Bheema listened carefully. Then he had
a word with his ministers. Everyone agreed
that Suku was right. This man Dhuri did
spread bad luck.

"Interesting," said the
king. "I wish to see him
tomorrow."

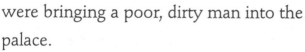

The next morning, while
the king was getting
dressed, he looked out
the window. The guards
were bringing a poor, dirty man into the
palace.

"Are you ready for the court, my dear?"
asked the queen.

The king turned swiftly and knocked over
a glass of water.

"Careful!" said the queen. "Don't be in
such a hurry."

When the king sat down for breakfast, he was told that the royal chef was not feeling well. So the king was unable to eat his favorite meal, *aloo paratha*—bread with spicy potato filling.

As the king approached the throne, he banged his leg and yelped in pain. Hurriedly he sat down, wishing that he had not peeped out the window that morning and looked at that man. He wished he had listened to his ministers, too. But he was the king. He had to meet everyone, even the man who spread bad luck.

"Bring in Dhuri," the king ordered.

Prince Veera and Suku stood behind the ministers and watched the proceedings. Suku shut his eyes tight and refused to look at the man even when Prince Veera nudged him.

"Dhuri, do you spread bad luck?" asked the king.

"I think I am filled with bad luck, Your Majesty," the man replied. "I have no work, no friends, and no family. But I don't believe I bring ill to anyone else."

"But that's not true," said the king. "I glanced at you early this morning from my window. I knocked over a glass of water, my favorite breakfast was not available, and I hurt my toes."

"Well, that could be carelessness, coincidence, and haste, Your Majesty."

"Are you calling me careless and hasty?"

"Not at all, Your Majesty. It happens to the best of us," Dhuri said. "Some days are better than others."

Prince Veera smiled. This man was intelligent, courageous, and articulate. It was unfortunate that no one gave him work.

"But I don't agree," said the king. "I agree with my ministers that you indeed spread bad luck. I condemn you to twenty-five years in prison so that no one will ever suffer again."

"That's not fair, Your Majesty," said Dhuri. "I didn't do anything wrong."

Prince Veera was shocked. He pulled Suku by his hand and stepped forward. "Father—Your Majesty," he began. "This is not fair."

"You are a child. Know your place," said the king.

"But you have always taught me to raise my voice against unfair things," said Veera. "This is one of them."

"This man spreads bad luck," the king said.

"But I can present to you another man who spreads more bad luck than Dhuri."

"Is there another one of these in my kingdom? Who is it?"

"You!" cried Prince Veera. "You have

managed to spread more bad luck than Dhuri."

Everyone in the court gasped. They looked at the prince with horror. Suku stepped back and moved behind the curtains.

"Veera, mind your words!" said the king.

"Please listen to me, Father. You glanced at Dhuri this morning and you had these minor accidents. You blame him for all your bad luck. But Dhuri didn't even look at you this morning. He was just coming over to see you. Yet you have sentenced him to twenty-five years in prison."

Dhuri looked up and smiled.

"If you believed Dhuri caused you hardship, then it is just superstition," said Veera. "Dhuri never intended to harm you. But what you did to

Dhuri is deliberate. You want him to rot in prison. It seems to me that you spread more bad luck and ill will than he does, Father."

King Bheema closed his eyes. He nodded slowly. Then he stepped down from his throne and hugged his son.

"You're right, my son. I was swayed by my emotions. I committed an injustice. Thank you for speaking the truth and speaking it loudly." The king walked back to his throne and looked at the court.

"Here in this court, we almost fell into the traps of superstition. I apologize to Dhuri for my hasty judgment."

"I am thankful to the prince, Your Majesty," said Dhuri. "And I am grateful to you for heeding to the voices in your court. May your rule flourish and prosper."

"Dhuri, you are a free man," said the king. "The minister will help you find a job and a place to stay."

The court adjourned and Suku peeped through the curtain. "You were very brave, Veera."

"I just stood up for the right thing," said Prince Veera. "That's what princes do."

A Jar of Pickles
and a Pinch
of Justice

To my mum, for her inspiration
and unconditional support
C. S.

Thanks, Jacky, two times lucky!
U. K.

Contents

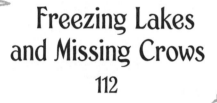

All's Well with
Mango Pickles

Long ago in a faraway land, King Bheema ruled a small kingdom surrounded by the magnificent hills of Himtuk. He was a kind and just ruler. He lived with his wife and his son, Prince Veera.

Prince Veera studied many subjects: the arts, mathematics,

science, economics, and languages, including Persian, Mandarin, and Latin.

Prince Veera's best friend, Suku, was not a royal. Suku had won the king's scholarship to study with the prince. He matched Veera's academic abilities and outdoor activities. Often the two boys competed in sports such as wrestling, archery, and horseback riding. When classes were over for the day, Prince Veera and Suku would wander through the markets and play in the mangroves.

One day during the previous summer, King Bheema had been unwell. Prince Veera and Suku offered to help out with his duties, and the king had allowed them to set up a court in the palace courtyard. There the boys listened to people's problems and solved petty disagreements.

Now the hot summer months were here once again.

"With no work to do on the farm and no classes," said Suku, "I'm bored."

"Maybe we can ask Father to invite us to the dance performances in the palace," suggested Prince Veera.

"Please don't," said Suku. "I can't sit in one place with a smile on my face for hours on end."

"That's my future you're describing!" said Veera. "What would you rather do instead?"

"We could set up court," Suku replied.

Prince Veera's eyes twinkled. "What a good idea," he said with a big grin. "Let's ask Father before he leaves for his hunting trip," he added, pulling Suku through the corridors.

When they entered the royal chambers, they found the king's room in a flurry. Attendants were packing bags, clothes were strewn everywhere, and King Bheema was pacing the floor.

"Is something wrong?" asked Suku.

"Packing is always traumatic," explained Veera.

"I can't find my hunting knife," said King Bheema, exasperated.

"It should be where you left it," said the queen from behind a cupboard. She, too, was looking for something.

"That's not very helpful," said the king. "Where did I leave it?"

Veera chuckled. His parents had the same conversation every time one of them left town.

"Did you two want something?" the king asked the boys.

"While you're away hunting," said Prince Veera, "we wondered if we could run the court in the courtyard."

"This boy is after my throne, I tell you," said King Bheema, smiling. "You may run the court as long as you don't bite off more than you can chew."

"We never do," said Prince Veera. "Thank you, Father. I wish you good fortune on your hunt."

"May the *vandevata,* the forest nymphs, help you along the way," said Suku.

As they left, a loud whoop came from the room. The king must have found his hunting knife, after all. The two boys rushed out to get ready for court the following day.

The next morning, a long line of people waited outside the palace to meet the king. When they found out that he was away, many of them were disappointed.

"Prince Veera is happy to listen to your problems," announced the guard.

Some people left, but many stayed to meet with the prince. They had heard wonderful things about his court.

Prince Veera summoned the first case. Two neighbors, Gopu and Dhanu, had come with a unique problem. Gopu had an old well in his overgrown garden, which he never used. Dhanu wanted to buy the well. A price was agreed on, and a document was drawn up: *I hereby sell just my well, situated behind my house, to Dhanu, my neighbor, for ten silver coins.*

The two men signed the document and Dhanu was happy to acquire the well in time for the summer.

"So what's the problem?" asked Suku. "You sold him the well, he bought the well, so all's well."

Prince Veera smiled at Suku's bad joke.

But he couldn't figure out the cause of their disagreement, either.

"I sold only the well, Your Majesty," said Gopu. "Not the water. So whenever Dhanu draws water from the well, he has to pay me half a silver."

Suku's jaw dropped open. Whoever heard of selling a well and charging for the water? Veera looked at Suku and raised his eyebrows.

"What do you say to that, Dhanu?" asked Prince Veera.

"Why would I buy just the well, Your Majesty?" asked Dhanu. "I need water for my garden during the summer months. But he wouldn't let me draw water from my own well unless I paid him half a silver."

"But you signed the document," said Gopu, waving a scroll in front of Dhanu. "It clearly says, 'just my well.'"

Suku reached for the scroll. What Gopu said was true. This was a tricky problem! Veera wanted to talk it over with Suku. They went to the garden for a walk.

"Why would someone buy a well and not the water?" asked Veera.

"If the well was empty, he could store his pots and pans in it," suggested Suku.

"Or maybe he has relatives coming and they need room to stay," said Veera.

"Next time you come to stay," said Suku,

"I'll ask them to prepare the well!"

"I'm sure you would join me, too," said Veera. "And maybe the well could be used as a hiding place." He was thinking about the hiding place his grandfather had made many years ago to escape from his enemies.

"The only trouble is," said Suku, "this well is not empty."

That's when Veera had an idea. "Come on, let's go," he said. "I know what to do."

"I've reached a decision," Prince Veera said, taking his seat in the courtyard.

Everyone was quiet. They wanted to know how the prince would solve this tricky case.

"According to the document, Dhanu bought only the well," said Prince Veera, "and not the water. Indeed, he should pay half a silver every time he draws water."

Gopu was overjoyed. *The prince is very astute,* he thought.

"But," Prince Veera continued, "he may have bought the well so that he could use it to store his belongings. Or perhaps he wants to live in the well."

Everyone was confused.

"As soon as the well was sold," explained Prince Veera, "Gopu should have removed the water."

"But, Your Majesty—" said Gopu.

"Shh!" warned Suku. Prince Veera wasn't finished.

"Gopu should take the water out of the well immediately or he should pay rent for storing the water in Dhanu's well."

Dhanu beamed. *The prince is indeed wise and just,* he thought.

Gopu hung his head in shame. The prince had outwitted him with his own trick. Gopu agreed not to charge Dhanu for the water lest he should be forced to pay for keeping the water in the well. The document was amended, and the prince warned Gopu not to try such a trick again.

"That was a little complicated," said Veera.

"It's water under the bridge now." Suku giggled.

"Seems like neighbors are not very nice to each other in our kingdom," observed Veera.

"That's why I live far away from the palace," said Suku. "You might not be a good neighbor."

Prince Veera chuckled. But he soon stopped, because the next man who came in was crying.

"Please," said Prince Veera. "Tell me your grievance."

"My name is Kasi, Your Majesty," said the man. "And I live next door to a man named Pawan."

"Are you crying because your name is Kasi or because you live next door to Pawan?" asked Suku.

"Neither," said Kasi. "I am crying because Pawan stole all my precious belongings." It seemed that neighborly feuds were not over for the day.

"We'll be the judges of that," said Suku. "Please state your case."

"My mother passed away a year ago," said Kasi. "I had to go to the holy city of Varanasi to perform her death ceremony."

Varanasi was a long way away. It took months to get there, even on horseback.

"Was the ceremony completed to your satisfaction?" asked Suku.

"Yes, it was," replied Kasi. "But before I left for Varanasi, I handed over a jar of pickles to my neighbor, Pawan, for safekeeping."

"It is important to keep pickles safe," said Prince Veera. He loved the tender mango pickles that Suku's mother made for him. He hid the jars in the royal kitchens so that he could eat the pickles all year.

"Actually, the jar didn't have any pickles in it," said Kasi. "I filled it with all my precious belongings—my gold ring, gold chain, silver coins, and even some rubies that had belonged to my mother."

"That's very clever," said Suku. "So what is the problem?"

"I didn't tell my neighbor that it was filled with valuables. He thought it was filled with pickles."

"Then what happened?" asked Veera. Thinking of pickles had made his mouth water.

"When I came back yesterday and asked for the jar," said Kasi, "Pawan returned my jar filled with pickles. My gold and silver and rubies were gone."

"Lemon or mango?" asked Veera.

Suku nudged Veera. Was that even important?

"It was filled with tender mango pickles," said Kasi. He started to cry again.

Every story had two sides. Prince Veera and Suku wanted to hear what Pawan had to say. Pawan was summoned to the court, but when he came before the prince, he didn't look worried.

"At your service, Your Majesty," he said.

"Your neighbor Kasi has lodged a complaint," said Suku. "He claims that you stole his gold and silver."

"And rubies," added Prince Veera.

"That's totally untrue," said Pawan. "I didn't steal his gold, silver, or rubies."

"Can you prove that?" asked Veera.

"Kasi gave me the jar for safekeeping

 before he left on his travels," said Pawan. "He repeatedly said that the jar contained tender mango pickles made by his mom before she died. He wanted me to keep it safe until he returned."

Veera and Suku turned to look at Kasi, who was still crying.

"When Kasi came back yesterday, I returned his jar of pickles," Pawan continued. "You can ask him what was in the jar."

"The jar was filled with tender mango pickles, Your Majesty," said Kasi.

"He gave me pickles and he got back pickles," said Pawan. "I never stole any gold or silver or rubies."

Prince Veera was confused. Yet another case that looked straightforward but wasn't. Was Kasi lying about the precious stones and silver and gold inside the jar, or had Pawan stolen everything and filled the jar with pickles?

It was almost lunchtime and Veera was hungry. All this talk of pickles was making him even hungrier.

"Let's finish this later," said Veera. "I need to think about it a little longer."

While the prince and his friend went to the royal dining hall, all the people waiting to see Veera were served lunch in the courtyard.

As they walked Veera said, "I don't know who is lying."

"Maybe instead of eating here we should go to my house for lunch," Suku suggested. "My mother knows everything about pickles."

"That's the best idea you've had all day!" said Prince Veera. He loved eating at Suku's house. Suku's mother was a wonderful cook. That day, she served them freshly made bread with spinach, potatoes, and lentils, and some fresh fish, too.

"How about some tender mango pickles to go with the fish?" she asked.

"Absolutely," chimed the boys in unison.

Veera bit into the fried fish and took a bite out of the tender pickled mango. Suku took a mouthful of rice mixed with the lentils, potatoes, and fish.

"Eat slowly," warned Suku's mother.

"It's so good, we can't wait between mouthfuls," said Veera.

"Tell me about your latest case," said Suku's mother. So they did.

Afterward, she said, "I don't know anything about justice, dear Veera. But I know something about pickles."

Suku's mother presented them with two cups of tender mango pickles.

"This one, on the right," she said, "was made this time last year."

Suku and Veera touched the mango pieces. They were shrunken and wrinkly. Suku bit into a piece. It was very chewy and salty.

"This one, on the left," she said, "the one you had for lunch today, was made last week. The mangoes were fresh from the trees and soaked two days after being picked."

These pieces were bright green, without wrinkles. Veera bit into one.

Crunch! The pickle was crunchy and the salt had not yet soaked into it.

Veera and Suku made their way back in silence. They were both busy thinking. The court was ready for them when they reached the palace. Before they entered, Suku said, "Are you thinking what I'm thinking?"

"Maybe," said Veera. "Are you thinking about crunchy pickles?"

"Maybe!"

As soon as Veera settled into his seat he said to Pawan, "I want to sample the pickles in the jar."

The guard placed the jar in front of the boys. The mango pieces were sloshing in the salt and chilly water. Suku took out two pieces of mango with a ladle.

The boys picked up one tender mango each and turned it around like they were looking at diamonds.

"Green!"

"Not wrinkly at all!"

"Let's try it," said Veera, and he bit into the piece. Suku did the same.

Crunch!

The mangoes were still fresh, like the ones they had eaten for lunch. These couldn't have been mangoes from last season. That meant Pawan had removed the contents of the jar and filled it with mangoes picked this season.

Pawan trembled as Veera glared at him. "You cheated your neighbor and stole his property," said Veera.

"And you thought we didn't know about pickles," said Suku.

Prince Veera confiscated all the stolen gold, silver, and rubies and returned them to Kasi.

Pawan was asked to work in the kitchens, making pickles for the rest of the season.

Kasi returned home, delighted that he had taken his case to the prince.

Prince Veera had one more thing to do: he talked to his father's minister and recommended that the palace organize a place of safekeeping, so that when people went away on long trips, they didn't have to worry about cheats and burglars. Something good for all the people would come out of something bad.

"This is an excellent idea!" said the minister. "You're surely taking after your father."

"Like mango, like pickle," said Suku. "That's what my mother always says."

Freezing Lakes
and Missing Crows

Prince Veera enjoyed running the court with Suku in the king's absence, even if they had to run it in the courtyard. He and Suku always had a good time. But after a week of listening to people complaining about friends, family, and neighbors, the boys wanted a break.

"Let's go to the riverbank," said Suku. "We could jump into the water and catch fish."

"And then we could go to the market and buy some palm fruits," said Prince Veera.

But just as they were changing out of their formal court attire, they heard news that King Bheema was on his way back home with a special guest. A welcome party was preparing to receive the king at the edge of the forest, where he was camping that night.

"The river will still be there tomorrow," said Veera. "Let's go and meet Father."

So the boys set off with the king's entourage. They took lots of food, fresh water and juice, and a band to play music.

The welcome party reached the king's camp by dusk. The king was overjoyed that Veera and Suku had come, too. He was eager to hear about their week running their own court.

"Who is your guest, Father?" asked Veera.

"Do you want to meet him now?" asked the king. "I thought it could wait until morning."

"I'm curious," said Veera.

"Don't say I didn't warn you," said King Bheema, and he sent word to the other tent.

Within a few minutes, the king and the two boys were invited there.

Veera gulped when he saw who was inside.

"Uncle, you remember Veera," said King Bheema.

"Welcome, Granduncle," said Prince Veera. "Are you passing through?"

"I've not visited my dear nephew in a long while," said Raja Apoorva, "and I have some family matters to discuss, too."

Oh no, thought Suku. This was the infamous uncle who handed out harsh punishments. The one who had never liked King Bheema or Prince Veera much. The palace walls were filled with gossip about Raja Apoorva.

Suku tried to blend in with the tent cloth. When he was introduced, Raja Apoorva just raised his right eyebrow as if to let King Bheema know that Veera was not keeping good company.

That night, after dinner, everyone sat outside their tents and chatted under the full moon.

"So what have you been up to?" Raja Apoorva asked Veera. "Surely you haven't been busy studying during the hot summer weeks?"

"We were running a court," said Prince Veera.

"What?" Raja Apoorva was surprised. Princes went on vacations in the hills during the summer.

As King Bheema proudly talked about the court cases from the previous year and how Veera had been courageous and just, Raja Apoorva shook his head.

"The prince is too young to listen to cases and bring justice to your people," he said.

"I have help," said Prince Veera. "Suku is very clever and knows about a lot of things."

Raja Apoorva grunted and ignored Suku completely.

The next morning, as the hunting party set off toward home, Raja Apoorva lagged behind, deep in thought. He had to show his nephew that the boys were not as clever as they thought and that a little knowledge was very dangerous.

When the king and his group reached the city, people stood on either side of the road to welcome him. The square got busier and busier as more people arrived. The king stopped to talk to a few people. Veera mingled, too.

"*Caw-caw!*" the crows crowed, and the people said, "The crows are signaling the arrival of our royal guests." This was a legend they had.

"Isn't that wonderful?" asked King Bheema. "Even the crows are happy that you're here. Indeed, your visit was long overdue."

"I've got a headache," said Raja Apoorva.

"Can you get someone to shoo the crows away, please?"

King Bheema sighed. He had been hoping to reach the palace without incident.

"They live here, too," said King Bheema. "Don't you remember the ancient stories? The crows have lived in our kingdom for centuries."

"Are you the king of the people or the crows?" asked Raja Apoorva. "In my kingdom, we culled all the frogs that croaked at night and all the crows that dirtied my beautiful bronze statues throughout the city."

"What's a little white decoration?" said King Bheema, trying to bring some humor into the conversation.

But Raja Apoorva wasn't listening.

"Maybe in honor of my visit," said Raja Apoorva, "you should cull all the crows."

Suku overheard this comment and bristled with anger. Whoever thought of culling birds and animals that lived in peace? They were as much a part of the city as the people. All night he had been angry about how Raja Apoorva had ignored him or smirked at him. Now the visiting king was insulting King Bheema, too.

King Bheema signaled the guards to guide the procession to the palace. It wasn't the time or the place to have an argument, especially with Raja Apoorva.

That evening, as the kings strolled in the garden, Veera and Suku joined them. A gentle breeze brought respite from the still-hot sun.

"Caw-caw!"

The harsh screech of the crows irritated Raja Apoorva again. "I told you," he said. "You've far too many crows in the capital and they disturb the royal peace.

Even if you don't want to cull all of them, you should cull at least some."

"How many is far too many?" asked Prince Veera. Crows and sparrows were part of the gardens. Who could think of them as a disturbance? He couldn't imagine a world without birds, butterflies, frogs, and fireflies.

"How many do you have in the capital?" asked Raja Apoorva. He was sure that the prince wouldn't be able to answer the question.

Veera blinked. "I don't know," he said. "With all due respect, Your Majesty, neither do you."

"Why don't you count the crows in the capital?" said Raja Apoorva. "Then we can have an informed debate."

Prince Veera knew this was a trap. The king was trying to make a fool out of him. Whoever heard of counting crows?

Sensing Veera's hesitation, Raja Apoorva chuckled. "I knew you would accept defeat at the merest mention of hard work," he said.

Suku tugged at Veera's sleeve. "Accept the challenge," he said. "We'll figure it out."

"Fine!" said Prince Veera. "Suku and I will count the crows by nightfall tomorrow."

King Bheema sat with his head in his hands. *Maybe a vacation for the boys would have been better,* he thought.

Suku stayed over at the palace that night and the boys kept busy trying to figure out how to count the crows.

"What about counting the crows in the garden and then multiplying that by the number of gardens in the city?" asked Veera.

"Maybe we could go for a walk in the morning and count all the crows we see," suggested Suku.

None of these ideas sounded right. They

could never count all the crows in a month, let alone one day.

"Perhaps we could tie a royal sign to all the crows we count," said Veera.

Suku started to giggle. "Imagine us running behind crows and getting pecked," he said. "The guards would be chasing the crows, too. And then the crows would poop on us."

"Even if we did that," said Veera, "there would be a problem. What if a crow without a royal sign came into the royal garden?"

"We would tell Raja Apoorva that this is a crow coming from another city," said Suku.

Veera's eyes sparkled. Suku had saved the day again. He hugged Suku and danced around the room.

"Are you going to tell me what's made you so happy?"

"I've got a plan to outwit Granduncle Apoorva and it is all because of your genius."

"How?"

"You'll find out soon enough," said Veera. That night he slept dreaming of crows pooping on Raja Apoorva.

The next morning, Veera and Suku went into town. After a long day strolling in the market, eating mangoes, and drinking lassi, they returned home just in time for the meeting with the kings.

"You are both covered in dust," said King Bheema.

"We've been busy counting crows," replied Prince Veera.

"Really?" said Raja Apoorva. "So did you manage to count all of them?"

"We never fail," said Prince Veera. "Suku will now read out the number."

Even King Bheema was curious. How did the boys manage it?

Suku pulled out a parchment from his pocket.

"Drumroll, please," said Prince Veera, smiling at Suku.

"We counted the crows in the gardens and markets, groves and swamps, and even the fields where the corn is being harvested," said Suku. "There are 75,325 crows in our capital city."

King Bheema wasn't sure whether to believe it or not. But Raja Apoorva was intrigued. How did they do it? *Surely the number is wrong,* he thought.

"What if I counted them and found more than 75,325 crows?"

"We knew you would ask that," said Prince Veera. "Crows are a very friendly species. Relatives and friends from other cities and kingdoms visit our crows. But to keep the counting accurate, we didn't count the visiting crows."

"You should reward them for their efforts," said King Bheema.

"Wait, wait," said Raja Apoorva. "One more question. What if I counted and there were fewer crows than the number you read out?"

"Your Majesty," said Suku. "The crows in our capital city have families far and wide in the kingdom. Some of them must have gone visiting."

King Bheema burst out laughing. "I hereby decree that the number of crows in our city is not excessive and there is no need to cull," he announced.

Raja Apoorva scowled, just for a second.

He realized that the two boys had beaten him at his own challenge.

Raja Apoorva clapped his hands and his guard brought a bag of gifts for the boys. "Well deserved," he said. "May you rule with wisdom always."

A few weeks later, summer was nearing its end. The monsoon season was not far away. The winds had turned strong and cold. The visiting king was due to leave in a couple of days. As a farewell gesture, King Bheema invited his uncle to grace the royal court. Raja Apoorva readily agreed.

Prince Veera and Suku had been invited to attend, too. Raja Apoorva watched the proceedings with great interest.

That afternoon, a poor man was brought before the king.

"My name is Omkar, Your Highness," said the man. "I never learned a trade or a skill and I didn't go to school. Now I'm unable to find a job so that I can feed my family."

King Bheema cleared his throat. But Raja Apoorva spoke first. "Dear nephew, Bheema," he said. "Would you allow me to hear this case?"

King Bheema hesitated for a moment and then nodded. "Of course," he said. "We would be delighted."

Veera looked at Suku and mouthed, "This is not good." But what could he do? His father had to respect the wishes of his uncle. That was an unwritten rule for all nephews.

Raja Apoorva wasted no time. He addressed the poor man in front of him. "Dear man, Omkar," he said. "What would you do to earn money for your family?"

"Anything, Your Highness," said Omkar.

"How about an unpleasant job?"

"Nothing is more unpleasant for me than to listen to my baby crying with hunger, Your Majesty," said Omkar. "I'm prepared to do anything."

"How do I know you're not just saying that?" asked Raja Apoorva. "I wish to test your words."

"I'll do anything, Your Majesty," repeated Omkar.

The man's suffering moved Veera and Suku. Families should not go hungry. Many times people had come asking for money and King Bheema would send them to the stables or the kitchens or the garden to get work. Perhaps Raja Apoorva would find the man a job that would provide him with a livelihood.

Raja Apoorva said, "This is what I want

you to do. I want you to stand by the royal
lake all night wearing nothing except your
dhoti."

The courtiers
gasped. Summer
was retreating.
The night would
be chilly and
windy.

But Omkar was
desperate. He agreed to the king's test.

"If you succeed," said Raja Apoorva,
"I will take you with me to my kingdom
and give you a job in the palace."

The court was dismissed in silence.
Many people were worried for Omkar.
Prince Veera and Suku knocked on King
Bheema's door.

"Father, this is unfair," said Veera. "You've
got to do something about it."

"We cannot interfere," said King

Bheema. "Omkar agreed, didn't he? If he had hesitated, I would have stepped in somehow."

"Your father is right," said Suku. "You've got to let Omkar prove to the world that he would do anything for his family."

"But if he dies?"

"The guards won't let that happen," said the king. "The royal doctor will be on hand."

Prince Veera wasn't convinced. But his father and Suku were right. They had to let Omkar try and win his fight with Granduncle, just as his father had let them count the crows.

That night, the boys watched from the palace windows. Omkar arrived with no shirt and no coat. He was wearing just a tattered dhoti. He stood on the banks of the lake, watched by two guards.

The moon climbed the sky and the oil lamps in the corridors and rooms were blown out. The palace slowly went to sleep.

Omkar was shivering in the cold, but he was determined to survive the night. He tried to distract himself by counting the columns in the palace corridors. Then he counted the fireflies.

The poor man was so cold that he was shaking. He tried to keep warm by rubbing his hands. He moved up and down the garden path surrounding the lake. Nothing helped.

Omkar hugged himself tight and looked at the sky. Even the moon was reluctant to watch him suffer. It hid behind the clouds. It was dark except for the light that flickered on the palace tower.

Omkar fixed his sight on the lamp. He imagined the flickering flame to be a raging fire. He imagined sitting before the fire and warming himself. He imagined roasting corn for his children.

As the guards rubbed their hands in the cold, Omkar was smiling. He was lost in his own imagination. He forgot about the cold wind and the mist that fell around him. All he could think about was the flame on top of the tower.

Slowly the moon moved away and let the sun return. At the crack of dawn, the guards took Omkar to the kitchen and gave him a warm drink and a blanket.

Soon it was time to go to the court. Omkar was confident that the king would give him a job and his family's suffering would be over. He was smiling even though he was still shaking from the cold. The courtiers had gathered early. Prince Veera and Suku had taken their places, too. Everyone eagerly awaited the kings' arrival.

Raja Apoorva was surprised to see Omkar in the court.

"So you didn't run away?" asked the king.

"Why would I, Maharaj?" asked Omkar. "I need the job."

"Did he have help to keep warm?" the king asked a guard.

"No, sir," said the guard. "He stood there all night in his dhoti with a smile on his face."

"Why were you smiling?" asked Raja Apoorva.

"I was gazing at the tower lamp, Your Majesty," said Omkar. "And imagined it to be a raging fire. In my imagination I was happily roasting corn in the fire for my children."

"Aha!" said Raja Apoorva. "You've had help. You were warmed by the tower lamp. You didn't complete this challenge as per the conditions I set out."

Omkar was stunned. How could the tower lamp warm him? It was so far away.

King Bheema bristled in anger. He had assigned this case to his uncle and couldn't interfere without insulting him. But it troubled him that one of his own citizens was not getting a fair hearing in his court.

Prince Veera and Suku, too, were outraged. How could Raja Apoorva treat the man with such callousness? Whoever heard of a lamp so far up in the tower warming a man by the lake? They had to do something. King Bheema shook his head slightly, warning them not to challenge Raja Apoorva.

Omkar was sent away from the court with nothing. King Bheema retired to his chambers, sullen and angry. As soon as the court was adjourned, the boys left the palace, too.

"What about Omkar?" asked Suku.

"I'm sure Father will help him after Granduncle has gone," said Veera.

"But we have to show Raja Apoorva that this is not fair," said Suku. "We cannot let him leave without a lesson."

"I agree," said Prince Veera. "I've been thinking the same thing."

That afternoon King Bheema didn't want to see Raja Apoorva. He wanted to eat with the boys. But the guards told him that Prince Veera was having lunch at Suku's house.

Raja Apoorva, too, was on his own. He gloated to his guards that he had saved himself a bundle of money because Omkar was a cheat. He was proud of his judgment, and proud that Prince Veera had learned a lesson in running a court.

It was the final evening of Raja Apoorva's visit. The kings met in the garden for a stroll.

"Where is Veera?" asked King Bheema.

"He hasn't returned from Suku's house, Your Majesty," said the guard.

"Why don't we go for a ride, Uncle?" asked King Bheema. "Veera must say good-bye to you."

"Why don't you summon him here?" asked Raja Apoorva.

"I thought you might like to see the city at night."

Raja Apoorva agreed, and the kings set off toward Suku's house.

As they dismounted their horses, Suku's father came out to greet them. "Welcome, Your Highnesses," he said. "I welcome both of you."

"Where is Veera?" asked King Bheema. "I want to see him right now."

"He's been cooking lunch all day, Your Majesty," said Suku's father.

"Cooking all day?" asked Raja Apoorva. "It's almost nightfall now. What kind of food is so special that he must cook all day?"

"He's just cooking rice, Your Majesty," said Suku's father. "Do come in."

The kings were curious. Why was Prince Veera cooking in Suku's house when a big pot of rice was always ready in the royal kitchens?

When they entered the kitchen, Raja Apoorva burst out laughing.

A stove was lit on the floor. A pot hung from the ceiling, far away from the heat.

"What are you doing, dear prince?" asked Raja Apoorva. "Surely you know how to cook rice? If not, do come to my palace and I will teach you personally."

"But I've learned this from you," said Prince Veera.

Suku giggled.

Raja Apoorva wasn't smiling, however. "What do you mean?" he demanded.

"You're a great monarch, Your Majesty," said Prince Veera. "For you even a tower lamp could warm a man by the lakeside. But I'm just a prince. I thought the blazing fire in the stove would heat the pot hanging just above it. That's not too much to ask, is it?"

King Bheema chuckled.

Raja Apoorva understood the prince's subtle message. The lamp in the tower was indeed too far away to warm the man by the lakeside. Omkar wasn't trying to cheat him. The poor man was desperate, and he had been turned away.

"You're very wise," said Raja Apoorva. "I'm humbled by the lesson you've taught me. I was wrong to dismiss Omkar for imagining the warmth from the lamp."

King Bheema hugged Prince Veera and

Suku. "I'm proud of you both," he said.
"I was so troubled by the judgment all day.
You've indeed brought me joy."

That night Raja Apoorva summoned
Omkar and his family. They were all fed
and clothed and asked to accompany the
king back to his kingdom. Omkar was given
a job at Raja Apoorva's palace. Omkar and
his family would never go hungry again.

"I bid you farewell, King Bheema," said
Raja Apoorva. "You must bring your son
and his friend to my palace next summer."

"As long as we don't have to count crows
or cook rice," said Prince Veera, "we'd be
delighted."

What's Fair?

It was a busy morning for Suku. He had agreed to help out in the fields before going to his classes with Prince Veera.

Suku's cousins and some neighbors were working alongside him. Everyone usually joked and laughed as they worked. Sometimes they sang, too. But this morning they were talking about the guard who stood outside the king's court. Suku inched closer to listen.

"He will take half of everything you would get," said one woman.

"Really? Does the king know?" asked the other.

"No one dares to complain about the king's guard to the king," said the first woman.

"How do you know it's true?" asked the second.

"My brother went to see the king and was given ten silver pieces to build a new hut," said the first woman. "The guard took five of those. My brother has hardly anything left to finish the hut now."

"That's terrible," said the second woman.

Suku agreed. It was terrible. How could a king's guard be dishonest and corrupt? He had to tell Veera at once.

That day, after classes, as they munched on spicy puffed rice, Suku told Veera about the conversation he had overheard. Veera, too, was upset. It was his father's court, after all. He had to do something about it.

"That's the new guard," said Veera. "He was appointed only a few days ago."

"New or old," said Suku, "he's not supposed to take anything from the people."

"Maybe we should tell Father," said Veera.

"We've no proof," said Suku.

"Then what should we do?" asked Veera. "We need to put this right."

"Maybe we should catch him red-handed." Suku paused and thought for a moment. "I've got a plan."

Veera listened as Suku outlined his idea. "That might work," said Veera. "Let's hope Father doesn't give the game away."

Veera quickly changed out of his expensive clothes and put on ordinary ones. He did this often when he and Suku visited markets and the village square. This time they were going to the royal court, pretending to be poor.

At the entrance there was a line. They watched the guard as he talked to each person before they entered the big hall where the court was held.

"Do you think he's discussing his chore?" asked Veera.

"Maybe," said Suku. "Or talking about the weather."

Veera chuckled. "For his sake, let's hope it is the weather."

The line moved slowly. Finally it was Veera's turn.

"What do you want?" asked the guard.
As he was new, he hadn't recognized the
prince and he didn't know Suku.

"We've come to see the king regarding a
job," said Suku.

"If you want me to let you
in," said the guard, "you must
promise to give me half of
what the king gives you."

"But . . ." said Veera.
"That's unfair."

"Standing here all day is
unfair," said the guard. "You give me my
share or I won't let you in."

"Please let us in," said Suku. "We promise
to give you half of everything we get."

"Clever boy," said the guard as he opened
the door.

King Bheema sat up in his throne in
surprise when he saw Veera and Suku enter.
But he didn't say anything. Veera always

had a reason for doing the things he did.

"State your case," said the usher.

"Your Majesty," said Veera, "we want to learn horseback riding and become soldiers. But we cannot afford to pay for riding lessons."

Veera can ride like the wind and so can Suku, thought the king. *What are the boys playing at?*

"We want to train in your stables, Your Majesty," said Suku.

"You want to train at the royal stables?" asked the king, playing along. "My stable is not a free school."

"But we don't have any money," said Veera. "And no one else would teach us."

"Nothing comes for free," said the king. "If you want to train in the stables, first you have to prove worthy of it."

"We'll do anything, Your Majesty," said Suku.

"You must work hard collecting the dung and cleaning the stables," said the king. "Then I'll let you train with my men."

"That's so kind of you, Your Majesty," said Veera. "There is just one more request."

"What's that?" asked the king. This was getting stranger by the minute.

"You have to let your guard come with us, too," said Veera.

"Why?"

"We promised to give him half of everything we got, Your Highness," said Suku.

"Why would you do that?" asked the king.

"If we didn't promise him half of what we got from you," said Veera, "the guard wouldn't let us in, Your Majesty."

"Summon the guard!" shouted King Bheema to his minister. How dare someone demand a bribe for letting people into the court?

The guard was brought before the king.

"Thank you, Veera and Suku," said the king. "You've indeed saved me from disgrace."

The court cheered for the boys, crying "Long live Prince Veera! Long live Suku!"

The guard realized his greed had landed him in big trouble. The king decreed that the guard would be sent to work in the stables. Stripped of his guard duty and all of his ill-gotten wealth, the guard would have to collect horse dung for a long time.

"It's good of you to take the farm gossip seriously," said Suku.

Veera shrugged. "Listening to what everyone says is part of the job," he said. "But now I want to play in the streets with you."

Suku was the king of street games—especially *gilli-danda*, the game of stick and stone. The boys set out to play near Suku's house. They rode their horses through the market square and past the village temple.

As always Veera's guards followed him at a discreet distance.

"Wait!" called out Suku.

"What?"

"Someone is sleeping on the temple steps," said Suku.

"He must be waiting for the temple to open," said Veera.

"I want to check," said Suku. "Maybe he's hungry or lost."

Veera followed him. The man had a tattered shawl draped over him and a dirty yellow cloth bag under his head.

"I think he's homeless," said Suku.

"But . . ." Veera hesitated. "I thought we provided homes to all homeless people."

"Perhaps he has come from another town, looking for work."

"Wake him up," said Veera. "Let's get him to a *choultry*. All travelers get food and shelter there, don't they?"

The guards woke the sleeping man.
As soon as he opened his eyes and saw the
guards, he tried to bolt.

"Don't be afraid," said Prince Veera.
"We mean no harm. We just want to help."

"No one can help me," said the man,
covering his face with a towel. "Please let
me go."

Prince Veera gestured to his guards to
wait on the street.

"Now that it's just the two of us boys,"
said Suku, "tell us why you're sleeping on
the temple steps."

"My name is Kalu," said the man. "I've
been running from one place to another ever
since I escaped."

"Escaped from where?" asked Veera.

"From Sheetalpur," said Kalu. "From King Athi's men."

"Why?" asked Suku. "Did you commit any crime?"

"My crime was my tickly nose," said Kalu. "All I did was sneeze at the wrong time."

Prince Veera was intrigued. What was this man's problem? How could a sneeze incur the wrath of King Athi?

Suku signaled to Veera to step aside.

"If he's running away from a royal punishment," said Suku, "your duty is to return him to King Athi of Sheetalpur."

"But—"

"King Athi could invade your kingdom if you give shelter to one of his prisoners," said Suku.

"But—"

"Veera, this is not *gilli-danda*," warned Suku. "You have to follow the royal charters of all the kingdoms around you, otherwise you'll put your own kingdom in danger."

But Veera wanted to find out more. How could sneezing be a crime?

"My dear Kalu," said Veera. "Tell us what happened."

"I worked for King Athi, looking after his royal attire and his chambers," explained Kalu. "We were all invited to his wedding."

"Did you steal anything?" asked Suku.

"Of course not," said Kalu. "I did the one thing that King Athi couldn't forgive."

"Did you eat his wedding cake?"

Kalu smiled sadly. "Maybe even that would not have caused my troubles," he said. "I sneezed just at the moment King Athi tied the sacred knot of marriage."

"What?" Suku gasped. "That was so inauspicious."

"Of course it was," said Kalu. "At least for me. King Athi thought it signaled an unhappy marriage and ordered his men to put me to death."

Veera bristled with anger. "No one should be put to death for sneezing," he said. "That's not fair."

"Didn't anyone try to help you?" asked Suku. He felt the same way as Veera, now that he had heard the man's story. How could they send him back to King Athi, who had been so rash and selfish?

"The new queen intervened," said Kalu. "She begged for mercy."

"Did that work?" asked Veera.

"A little," said Kalu. "The king allowed me to choose how I wanted to die. But die I must, he said."

"That's terrible," said Veera.

"I escaped from the wedding hall," said Kalu. "And I've been running ever since."

"Maybe King Athi will have cooled down by now?" asked Suku.

"No chance of that," said the man, showing a parchment with his name and a reward for catching him written on it.

Suku and Veera sat down on the temple steps. They had to send the man back to Sheetalpur. But they didn't want him to be put to death, either. Was there another way?

"Maybe he should choose poison," said Suku. "That would be quick."

"You're not helping," said Veera.

"Maybe he should be trampled by an elephant?" asked Suku.

"Don't be like that," said Veera.

"Maybe every day for a month he could read the stories you write," said Suku. "That would kill him for sure."

"Very funny," said Veera. "Maybe he could read your poems. That would kill him instantly."

"It hasn't killed you," said Suku.

"That's because I've become immune to them," said Veera. At that moment, something clicked in his head.

"Maybe—" began Suku.

"Wait a moment," said Veera. "I think I've found a way to save Kalu."

"What's that?" asked Suku.

"Kalu, you could die of old age," said Veera. "That would satisfy the king's decree and let you live until you are old."

Kalu's eyes lit up. That was perfect. The boys had saved his life.

"You're a genius," said Suku. "But he

should stop going to weddings or sneezing, or both, until he's really old."

Veera instructed his guards to take Kalu back to Sheetalpur. Kalu was confident of escaping King Athi's wrath and relieved to be going back home to see his family.

"Now, it's time I beat you at *gilli-danda*," said Suku.

"I may beat you today," said Veera.

"Not a chance—not even when you're old and wrinkled," said Suku, riding ahead.

Gray Elephants
and Five Fools

Suku's aunt Chandra was a washerwoman. While she worked, she sang songs about the forests and the trees, the rivers and the bees. People in the village often stopped outside her house to listen. Like all washerwomen, she had a donkey.

The donkey carried her load to and from the river and sang with her whenever it pleased. But of course the donkey's braying was not sweet like Chandra's voice. Like any other donkey's, its braying was loud and harsh.

One evening, Suku saw his aunt Chandra in the market.

"Hello, Aunt Chandra," said Suku. "How are you today?"

"Same old, same old," said Chandra. "Every day I get into a fight with the potter next door."

"Why?" asked Suku.

"The potter gets upset about everything I do: 'You beat your clothes too loudly,' he says. 'Your donkey brays too loudly; your singing is horrible.'"

"But you sing beautifully," said Suku. "That man must have no taste."

"Mark my words, nephew," said Chandra, "one day that potter is going to bring lots of trouble and drop it on my doorstep."

"I hope that doesn't happen," said Suku. "But if it does, I'll be there to help you."

One day, the potter was working on a vase for a rich man. It was a special order worth a lot of money. The potter had spent hours preparing the clay and setting it up on his potter's wheel. He didn't want anything to go wrong.

The clay was poised on the wheel as it began to spin. Slowly, the vase began to take shape in the potter's deft hands. Just when he was curving his fingers to shape the neck of the vase, he heard *"Hee-haw! Hee-haw!"*

The potter was so startled that he let go of the vase. Now it lay splattered on the ground in a big lump. He would have to start all over again. The potter was enraged at the donkey and at the washerwoman, who had allowed the donkey to sing. "No one should encourage donkeys to sing," he mumbled. "Enough is enough. I'm going to get rid of the woman and her donkey once and for all."

That night he lay awake plotting an evil plan.

Early the next morning, the potter stood in the line to meet King Bheema.

"What can I do for you?" asked the king.

"I have not come to ask for help, Your Majesty," said the potter. "I have come to help *you*."

The king was astonished. How could the man possibly help him? Was he a spy? A wise man with advice? Or an astrologer with a prediction for the forthcoming year?

"Do tell me," said King Bheema. "I'm intrigued."

"I'm a potter, Your Majesty," said the man. "I saw Airavata, the celestial elephant

that belongs to Indra,
the god of thunder,
in my dreams."

"I hear that's a
good omen," said the
king, still unsure why the
man was in his court.

"Yes, Your Majesty," said the potter. "But
I wondered why that dream came to me.
That's when I realized it wasn't for me. I
don't have any elephants. The gods were
sending a message to you through me."

"And what message would that be?"
asked the king.

"Even though your royal elephants are tall
and strong," said the potter, "they are still as
gray as the monsoon clouds."

The king wasn't sure if the man was
insane or genuinely trying to help. He
decided to listen to him—after all, that's
why he kept the doors to his court open.

"What should I do?" asked King Bheema.

"I know someone who can wash your elephants and turn them as white as Airavata," said the potter.

"Really?" said the king. "Who is that?"

"My neighbor, the washerwoman Chandra," said the potter. "She could turn even the grayest of clothes white. She would be perfect for the job."

The king was amused. Who was this miracle woman who could turn his elephants from gray to white? Was the potter trying to get a job at the palace for his neighbor?

"Bring the washerwoman to my court tomorrow," ordered the king.

When the news spread about the potter's dream and his suggestion to the king, everyone was afraid for Chandra. How could she change the color of the elephants?

Soon the rumors reached Chandra, too.

She was worried. She had known the day would come when the potter would bring her harm. What was she going to do? *Maybe Suku could help,* she thought. Suku visited the king often and was friends with the prince. Maybe Suku could tell the king about the potter's ploy.

Chandra went to Suku's house and explained the situation. "Tell me how to get out of this," she begged.

"Don't worry, Aunt Chandra," said Suku. "I'll come up with something."

Suku didn't waste a moment. He set off to the palace to see Prince Veera.

"I need your help, my friend," said Suku. He told Veera about the tiff between the potter and his aunt and how it had reached the palace.

"I don't like this at all," said Veera. "It is one thing to have a disagreement with a neighbor; everyone does."

"We have seen so many cases of that," agreed Suku. He recalled the neighbors fighting about wells and water, mango pickles and precious gems.

"But to bring it to the king and make him party to their feud," said Prince Veera, "well, that's crossing the line."

"And she is my aunt," said Suku. "I need to help her."

"I'm sure Father will be fair," said Veera. "We should teach the potter a lesson, though."

Suku agreed. They couldn't just complain about the potter to the king. They needed a plan.

"Can you show me how your aunt washes clothes?" said Veera.

"Like everyone else, I suppose," said Suku.

"I have never washed my own clothes," said Veera. "So show me."

Suku took Veera back to his aunt's house

in the village. She had bundles of dirty clothing to wash.

"I soak the clothes in big pots, like this," explained Chandra. "Then I beat them on a stone. After that I wash them in the river and dry them on the riverbank."

Veera watched with fascination. *I should learn about all the trades in my kingdom,* he thought. Now every time he put on clean clothes, he would appreciate the work that went into washing them.

"What if you had to wash a big blanket?" asked Veera.

"I would need a bigger pot," said Chandra. "I would get one from the market.

The potter next door has a shop there."

Veera smiled. "I think I know how to outwit the potter," he said. "But you must do what I tell you." Then Veera explained his plan to Suku and Chandra.

That night Chandra slept peacefully. She knew the prince's idea would save her from the wrath of the king and perhaps even stop the potter from bothering her again.

Early the next morning, the king summoned the washerwoman to the court. Prince Veera and Suku were there, too.

"I order you to wash my elephants and turn them white, just like Airavata, the celestial elephant in the skies," said King

Bheema. He was sure the woman would refuse. Who could do such a task?

The washerwoman didn't seem perturbed at all. She smiled at the king and said, "Of course, Your Majesty. May I see your elephants first?"

The king was taken aback.

"Perhaps we should invite the potter, too, to come with us to the stables," said Prince Veera. "After all, it was his dream."

The king agreed, and the potter was summoned. When he arrived, he joined the king and his entourage as they walked to the stables with Chandra, Veera, and Suku.

Chandra entered the stables. She walked around the first elephant. She took out a string and measured the elephant. She touched its back and its trunk. Then she repeated the same process with the second elephant. She pursed her lips, nodded, and muttered to herself.

The king
watched with
amusement as
she considered
the task. Suku
and Veera were
watching the potter. He looked far
more afraid than the washerwoman.

Finally, after a few minutes of inspection,
Chandra stepped out of the stables. She
looked at the king solemnly and said, "I
think I can wash these elephants and turn
them white, Your Majesty."

"What?" the king exclaimed in surprise.

"But I need a few supplies before I can get
to work."

"What do you need?" asked Veera.

"I need two pots to soak
each of these elephants in,"
she said. "The pots need
to be big and strong

enough to hold the elephants overnight."

The king caught on quickly. He looked at Veera and Suku, who were grinning from ear to ear.

The king turned to the potter and said, "Dear man, your idea was wonderful. Now I am relying on you to make the biggest, strongest pots to soak my elephants in."

The potter gasped. His mouth fell open in shock. "B-but . . ." he stammered.

"Come with the pots," said the king, "as soon as you can."

The potter ran from the stables back to his house. He packed his bags and left the village, lest the king should send soldiers asking for the pots.

Chandra left the palace happy. She had managed to thwart the potter's ploy.

"So tell me, boys," said the king. "Did the washerwoman have any help?"

Suku nodded and pointed at Veera. "She is

my aunt, Your Majesty," he said. "And I'm grateful to Veera for helping me."

"I knew it," said the king. "Well done!"

That night the village celebrated the potter's defeat and Chandra's victory with a big feast. The guests of honor were Prince Veera and his best friend, Suku.

A few days later, a poet was invited to the king's court. It was customary for visiting

poets to recite some
verses in honor of
the king and his
kingdom. The king would
then reward the poet with
money and perhaps even a title.

The poet spent the whole morning reciting
poems about the king's generosity. The
king rewarded him with a lavish lunch with
himself and his courtiers. In the afternoon,
the poet recited poems about how the
kingdom was filled with clever people. He
read out many verses exalting the wisdom
of not just the king and his court, but every
citizen in the kingdom.

Prince Veera and Suku listened to the last
few verses from the balcony upstairs. "The
poet is very talented," said Suku.

"He exaggerates," said Prince Veera. "He's
just trying to impress Father."

"It's not so easy to impress you," said Suku.

That evening, after the poet had set off on his journey with a cart full of gifts, the king was in a good mood.

"I agree with the poet," said the king. "Our kingdom is filled with wise men and women. We have no fools."

Prince Veera nudged Suku. "I told you," he whispered. "The poet has given Father a high horse."

"What horse?" asked King Bheema, catching the last word in Veera's sentence.

"You shouldn't believe everything the poet said, Father," said Veera. "He used the word *wise* just to rhyme with *nice*."

"I'm not that naïve," said the king. "I sincerely believe I don't have any fools in my kingdom."

"What if I prove you wrong?" said Veera. "Suku and I will make our way through the village and find five fools. We'll meet you at the palace gardens in an hour."

The king smiled. "You're bored, I think," he said. "I challenge you to find a single fool, let alone five."

Veera and Suku set off toward the village. On their way, they met a woman who was searching for something in the river.

"What are you looking for?" asked Suku.

"My gold ring," said the woman.

"When did you lose it?" asked Suku.

"This afternoon, when I was working."

"Where were you working?" asked Suku.

"In the mangrove," said the woman.

"Why are you looking in the river if you lost the ring in the mangrove?" asked Prince Veera.

"You're so silly," said the woman. She had not recognized the prince. "The mangrove is dark now. But the river is well lit. There's a better chance of finding the ring here."

"Come with me," said the prince. "We'll get someone to find your ring for you tomorrow."

So the woman followed the boys as they walked to the village.

On their way, they met a farmer on a donkey, with a bundle of firewood on his head.

"Dear man," said Prince Veera, walking alongside the donkey. "Why don't you place the firewood on the donkey's back?"

The man was aghast at the suggestion.

"Can't you see my donkey is very tired?" asked the man. "How can I burden it with the firewood, too?"

Prince Veera invited the man to join them. Suku offered to carry the firewood until they reached the palace.

As the party of four made their way through the village, they saw a man lying on his back in the street. His hands were in the air and he was calling out to people to help him get up.

What is he doing? wondered Prince Veera.

Suku placed the bundle of firewood on the ground and asked the man about his predicament.

"Can't you see my hands are far apart?" answered the man. "How can I get up without moving them?"

"Why are you holding them apart?" asked Suku.

"Because that's the length of the fabric my wife asked me to bring from the shops."

"Why are you on the ground, then?" asked Prince Veera. "Surely the fabric shop is not down there?"

"I slipped on a banana peel and fell," said the man. "I can't get up without moving my hands. And if I move my hands, I'll forget the measurement."

Prince Veera and Suku helped the man up without holding his hands and asked that he, too, come with them.

"Our job is done here," said Veera. "Let's go to the palace."

"But . . ." said Suku. They had only three fools with them. Veera had promised the king he would find five.

"Trust me," said Veera.

Suku smiled. Veera must have something up his sleeve.

When they reached the palace, the king was pacing in the gardens impatiently.

"There you are," he said. "I'm sure you found no fools in my kingdom."

"I found five soon enough, Your Highness," said Veera.

The king looked at the woman who was crying for her ring, the farmer on the donkey, and the man with his hands held far apart. Veera explained why he had brought them.

"There are only three," said the king. "Have you failed?"

"You haven't counted all the fools," said Veera. "In addition to the three I brought, you already know the other two."

The king looked puzzled.

"The fourth fool is me, Your Majesty, for going on an errand to fetch fools," said Veera. "And the fifth fool is you, who got taken in by the words of the poet and believed that your kingdom could have no fools."

Suku gasped. Had Veera crossed the line? He had just called the king a fool!

The king was silent. The garden was quiet except for the call of the birds returning home to roost.

Suddenly the king erupted into laughter,

startling the three people that Veera had brought to the palace. "You're right, as usual, my dear son," said the king. "I was blinded by the praise of the poet. I had forgotten that it takes all sorts to make a kingdom. We can't all be brave, wise, and funny."

"Yes, Your Majesty," said Prince Veera. "No one is wiser than you."

That evening as they walked back to the palace, Prince Veera hoped that he, too, would be as humble and wise as his father and that his best friend, Suku, would be by his side to point out his faults without fear.